Rumpelstiltskin

Retold by Vera Southgate M.A., B.COM
with illustrations by Frank Endersby

LADYBIRD TALES

ONCE UPON A TIME there was a poor miller who had one beautiful daughter.

One day, the king sent for the miller. When the miller stood before the king, he was rather frightened.

Instead of remaining quiet, the foolish man said the first silly thing that popped into his head. "My daughter can spin straw into gold," he said.

"Your daughter is indeed clever if she can do as you say!" answered the king. "Bring her to me tomorrow and we shall see."

The next day the miller took his daughter to the king's castle.

The king led the girl into a room that was filled with straw. The only other things in the room were a stool, a spindle and some reels.

"Now set to work," said the king, "and, if by tomorrow morning you have not spun this straw into gold, you must die!"

At these words, the king left the room and locked the door behind him.

The miller's daughter sat down on the stool and gazed at all the straw. She didn't know what to do. She had no idea how to spin straw into gold. She hid her face in her hands and wept.

All at once the door flew open and in came the strangest little man she had ever seen.

"Good evening, Mistress Miller," said the tiny man. "Why are you crying?"

"Alas!" replied the girl. "I have to spin all this straw into gold and I do not know how."

"But I do!" said the little man. "What will you give me if I spin it for you?"

"My necklace," replied the girl.

The little man took the necklace and sat down in front of the spinning wheel.

Whirr, whirr, whirr; three times round and one reel was full. The little man put on another reel.

Whirr, whirr, whirr; three times round and the second reel was full. And so it went on all night.

By morning all the straw was spun and all the reels were full of gold. Whereupon the little man disappeared.

At sunrise the king arrived. He was both astonished and delighted to see so much gold. Yet he wasn't satisfied. The sight of the gold only made him more greedy.

He took the miller's daughter to a second room, much larger than the first one. It, too, was full of straw.

Again the king told the girl that if all the straw was not spun into gold before next morning, she must die.

Once more, when she was left alone, the girl began to cry.

In a moment the door flew open and the little man stood before her.

"What will you give me if I spin this straw into gold?" asked the little man.

"The ring on my finger," replied the miller's daughter.

The little man took the ring. He sat and spun the straw all night until all the reels were full of gold. Then once more he disappeared.

The king arrived at sunrise and again he was delighted to see all the gold. Yet still he wasn't satisfied.

He led the poor girl to a third room, even larger than the other two. It, too, was full of straw.

This time the king said to the girl, "Spin this straw into gold before morning and you shall be my queen."

When the girl sat alone, weeping, the strange little man appeared again.

"What will you give me if I spin the straw for you?" he asked.

"Alas! I have nothing to give," sobbed the poor girl.

"Then promise me that, if you become Queen, you will give me your first child," said the little man.

"I may never become Queen nor yet have a child," thought the girl. So she promised. At that, the little man spun all the straw into gold.

When the king arrived, early the next morning, he was overjoyed at the sight of all the gold.

He reminded himself that, not only was the miller's daughter beautiful, but also that she had brought him great riches.

So he kept his promise. He married the miller's daughter and she became his queen.

The queen was very happy, living
in the royal castle. She forgot all about
the little man who had spun the straw
into gold.

A year after they were married, the
king and queen had a lovely baby. They
were both filled with joy.

A few days later, the little man suddenly appeared in the queen's bedroom.

"Now give me what you promised," he said to the queen, as he pointed to the sleeping baby.

The poor queen was horrified and clutched her baby tightly.

The queen offered the little man all the riches of her kingdom, if only he would release her from her promise.

The little man refused them all.
"A human child would be dearer
to me than all the riches of your
kingdom," he said to the queen.

At these words, the queen wept so
bitterly that the tiny man took pity
on her.

"I will give you three days," he said,
"and if in that time you can guess my
name, you shall keep your child."

That night the queen lay awake, trying
to remember every name she had
ever heard.

In the morning the queen sent for a
messenger. She told him to ride all over
the country, collecting all the boys'
names he could find.

When the little man came the next day, the queen repeated her long list of names. But after each name the little man said, "No, that isn't my name."

The next morning the queen sent her messenger to another country. He came back with a long list of the strangest names she had ever heard.

The queen repeated all these strange names to the little man on his second visit. After each name he shook his head and said, "No, that isn't my name."

The poor queen was in despair.

On the third day, it was very late when the messenger returned.

"I haven't been able to find any new names," he said, "but, as I came to a high mountain, at the end of the forest, I saw a little house. In front of the house, there was a fire burning."

"The strangest little man was
hopping and jumping round the fire,"
went on the messenger, "and this is
what he was singing:

Although today I brew and bake,
Tomorrow the queen's own child
  I'll take.
This guessing game she'll
  never win,
For my name is Rumpelstiltskin."

On hearing this, the queen clapped her
hands with joy.

When the little man arrived, the queen pretended she still didn't know his name.

"Is your name Twinkletoes?" she asked.

"No, that isn't my name," he replied.

"Is it Shagribanda?" she asked.

"No, that isn't my name," he replied.

"Does it happen to be Rumpelstiltskin?"

The little man was furious.
"A witch has told you! A witch has told you!" he shrieked, as he stamped his feet in anger.

He stamped so hard that his right leg went through the floor. At that, his anger increased. He seized his leg with both hands and pulled with all his might until he was free.

Then Rumpelstiltskin stomped furiously out of the room and was never heard of again.

The king, queen and their child lived in happiness and peace from then on.

A History of Rumpelstiltskin

As with many fairy tales, *Rumpelstiltskin* has inspired songs and films. Most recently, the character has appeared in the popular *Shrek* films.

The story of *Rumpelstiltskin* has existed for centuries and many versions have been written. The fairy tale is well-known throughout Europe and has been studied by many folklorists.

The Brothers Grimm collected the various tales and turned them into the popular version of the story that we are familiar with today. *Rumpelstilzhen*, as it was called, was first published in the 1812 edition of *Children's and Household Tales*.

Variations on a mischievous dwarf like Rumpelstiltskin have appeared over the years, including Tom Tit Tot, Terrytop and Whuppity Stoorie.

Vera Southgate's 1968 retelling has boosted the popularity of the story and helped to ensure that it continues to be well-known and much-loved.

Collect more fantastic
LADYBIRD 🐞 TALES

Cinderella

Hansel and Gretel

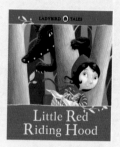
Little Red Riding Hood

The Three Little Pigs

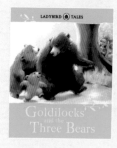
Goldilocks and the Three Bears

The Gingerbread Man

Snow White and the Seven Dwarfs

Rapunzel

Rumpelstiltskin

Sleeping Beauty

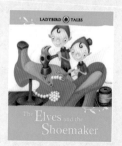
The Elves and the Shoemaker

Puss in Boots